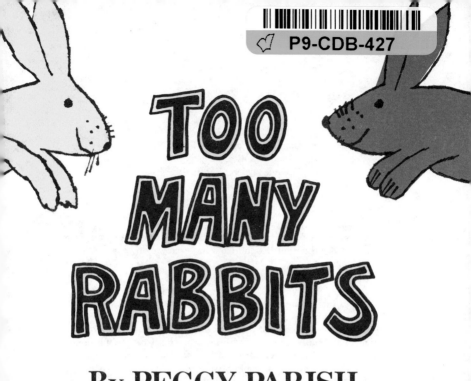

TOO MANY RABBITS

By PEGGY PARISH
Pictures by LEONARD KESSLER

A Young Yearling Book

Published by
Bantam Doubleday Dell Books for Young Readers
a division of
Bantam Doubleday Dell Publishing Group, Inc.
1540 Broadway
New York, New York 10036

ISBN: 0-440-40591-2

Reprinted by arrangement with the artist and the estate of the author

Printed in the United States of America

April 1992

10   9   8   7

For
Dr. Stephen Gushin
with much
gratitude
and
affection

Thump! Thump! Thump!

"Now what is that?"

said Miss Molly.

Thump! Thump! Thump!

"There it is again,"

said Miss Molly.

"I had better see what it is."

Miss Molly went to her door.

She opened it.

There sat a fat rabbit.

"Goodness me!" said Miss Molly.

"Where did you come from?"

The rabbit looked at Miss Molly.

Then she looked at the open door.

"Oh, well," said Miss Molly.

"Come in if you like."

But the rabbit was already in.

"I will feed you," said Miss Molly.

"Then you must go home."

So Miss Molly fed the rabbit.

"All right," she said.

"Out you go."

She opened the door.

But the rabbit hopped the other way.

"So you came to stay," said Miss Molly.

"Well, you may stay tonight.

But tomorrow you must go.

I will fix a box for you."

And she did.

The rabbit hopped into the box.

Miss Molly went to bed.

Soon she was asleep.

Next morning Miss Molly got up.

She went to the kitchen.

The rabbit was still in the box.

"Did you have a good night?"

said Miss Molly.

The rabbit said nothing.

"Here is your breakfast,"

said Miss Molly.

The rabbit did not move.

"You are a lazy one," said Miss Molly.

She went over to the rabbit's box.

And what a surprise she had.

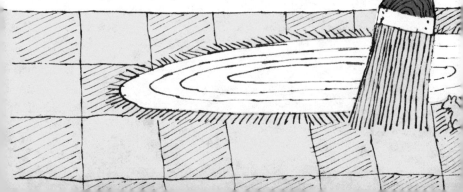

She saw not one rabbit.

She saw a box full of them.

"Oh, dear!" said Miss Molly.

"Baby rabbits! Lots of baby rabbits.

No wonder you wanted to stay."

Miss Molly shook her head.

"Babies need lots of care.

Even baby rabbits.

I will have to let them stay,"
she said.

So all of the rabbits stayed.

It wasn't much bother at first.

The babies only needed milk.

And their mother had plenty of that.

But rabbits grow fast.

Soon they wanted real food.

Miss Molly had to buy it for them.

Carrots and lettuce and corn.

Cabbage and apples and turnips.

"My," said Miss Molly.

"My rabbits eat more than I do.

I must do something.

Maybe I should get rid of some rabbits."

Then she looked at them.

"But they are so cute," she said.

"And they are still little."

So she kept all of them.

But the rabbits did not stay little.
Before long they were everywhere.
They were on the chairs
and under the chairs.
They were on the bed
and under the bed.
They were even in the bathtub.
"Oh, dear!" said Miss Molly.

"I have too many rabbits.

They are grown up now.

I really should get rid of them."

She thought about it.

Then she shook her head.

"No," she said. "I can't do that.

I like my rabbits."

So she kept them all.

Then one morning Miss Molly
had a BIG surprise.
"Oh, no!" she said.
"More baby rabbits!
Whatever will I do?"
Miss Molly could not decide.
So she did nothing.
And the new little rabbits grew.
Rabbits were everywhere.
They were on the chairs
and under the chairs.
They were on the bed
and under the bed.
They were in the bathtub
and in the laundry basket.

Miss Molly could hardly walk around.

Then one day she opened the bread box.

Out popped a rabbit.

"That does it!" she said.

"I've had quite enough.

These rabbits must go."

Miss Molly looked out of a window.

She saw a boy.

"Tommy," she called.

"Do you like rabbits?"

"Oh, yes!" said Tommy.

"Do your friends like rabbits?"
said Miss Molly.

"Sure," said Tommy.

"Everybody likes rabbits."

"Good," said Miss Molly.

"Go get your friends.

I have rabbits for all of you."

"Yippee!" said Tommy.

He ran off.

"Now that was a good idea,"
said Miss Molly.

"Children love pets.
They will be good to my rabbits."

Miss Molly sat down to wait.

Soon her doorbell rang.

She opened the door.

There were piles of children.

"Do come in," said Miss Molly.

"You may choose your rabbits."

Some children chose one rabbit.

Some chose two.

Some even chose three.

Every rabbit was taken.

And every child was gone.

Miss Molly bustled around.

She cleaned and cleaned.

Soon her little house sparkled.

Miss Molly made herself a cup of tea.

"How nice it is to be alone," she said.

Then the doorbell rang.

Miss Molly went to the door.

There were piles of children.

And piles of rabbits.

Each child said,

"My mama said 'no.'"

Again there were rabbits everywhere.

"Oh, dear!" said Miss Molly.

"Now what shall I do?"

She thought about it.

Then she nodded.

"The zoo," she said.

"They have lots of animals.

I will give them my rabbits."

So Miss Molly called the zoo.

But the zoo said "no."

They did not need any rabbits.

And everywhere Miss Molly stepped
there was a rabbit.
Something had to be done.
Miss Molly thought
until she went to sleep.
Then she woke up with an idea.

"I will put an ad in the paper,"
she said.

And she did.

It said RABBITS FOR FREE.

Then Miss Molly waited.

Finally the doorbell rang.

It was the butcher.

"I will take those rabbits," he said.

"All of them?" said Miss Molly.

"Yes," said the butcher.

"Lots of people like rabbit meat."

"No, no, no!" said Miss Molly.

"My rabbits are pets.
Nobody is going to eat them."
She slammed the door.

The next day the doorbell rang again.

Miss Molly opened the door.

A man stood there.

A big truck was parked outside.

"I would like your rabbits,"
said the man.
"Are you going to eat them?"
said Miss Molly.
"Oh, no!" said the man.
"What will you do with them?"
said Miss Molly.

"I have an island," said the man.

"It has grass and trees.

It even has a stream.

But it has no rabbits.

And I like rabbits."

"Grass, trees, a stream,"

said Miss Molly.

"My rabbits would like that."

Then she nodded.

"You may have my rabbits," she said.

So they loaded the truck with rabbits.

Miss Molly waved good-by to them.

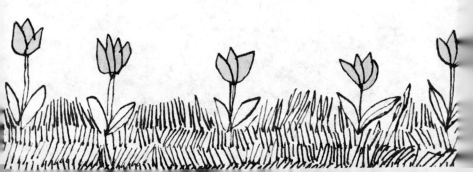

Something rubbed against her leg.

Miss Molly looked down.

There was a fat gray cat.

"Now I've always wanted a cat,"
said Miss Molly.

"You may come in.

A cat is no trouble."

Miss Molly went to bed happy.

Her rabbits had a good home.

And she had a nice new pet.

Next morning Miss Molly got up.

She went to the kitchen.

The cat was still in the box.

"Did you have a good night?"
said Miss Molly.

The cat said nothing.

"Here is your breakfast,"
said Miss Molly.

The cat did not move.

"You are a lazy one," said Miss Molly.

She went over to the cat's box.

And Miss Molly threw up her hands.

"Oh, no!" she said.

For that box was filled with kittens.

"I do have problems," said Miss Molly.

"I wonder if that man
with an island likes cats?"

Then Miss Molly shook her head.

"But I will have to grow them up first.

Babies do need lots of care.

And these are so cute."

Miss Molly smiled.

Then she went to heat some milk

for the mother cat.